RIDDLES FROM
THE HOPE CHEST

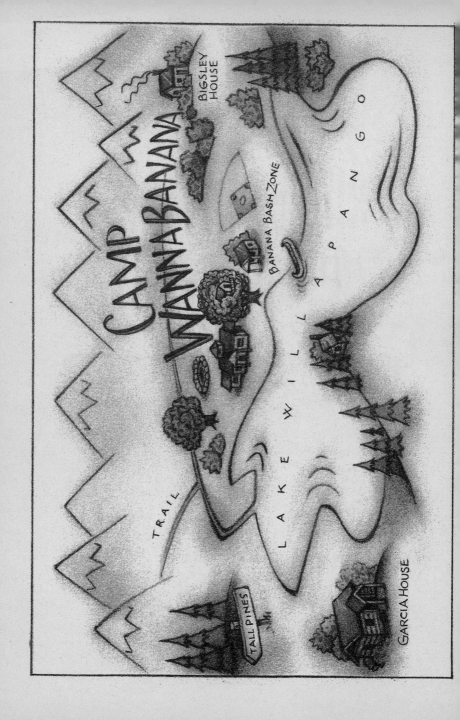

CAMP
WANNA BANANA
MYSTERIES

RIDDLES FROM THE HOPE CHEST

Becky Freeman

WaterBrook
PRESS

RIDDLES FROM THE HOPE CHEST
PUBLISHED BY WATERBROOK PRESS
2375 Telstar Drive, Suite 160
Colorado Springs, Colorado 80920
A division of Random House, Inc.

ISBN 1-57856-353-4

Published in association with the literary agency of Alive Communications, Inc.,
7680 Goddard Street, Suite 200, Colorado Springs, CO 80920.

Printed in the United States of America
2002—First Edition

10 9 8 7 6 5 4 3 2 1

To the youngest Sugar 'n' Spice in our family tree,
who decorate my world with feminine charm:
my daughter, Rachel,
my daughter-in-love, Amy,
and my little niece, Tori Leigh.

CONTENTS

ACKNOWLEDGMENTS

Thank you to Erin Healy, editor extraordinaire. You have been the other half of my brain in making this a wonderful series. I can't believe we are finished with the fifth book! Jake, Joy, Marco, Maria—and of course, Munch-Munch—almost feel like part of my family now.

Also, to my agent, Greg Johnson, who helps make so many of my writing dreams come true. Gratitude to WaterBrook and Children of Faith for all you will do to get these books into the hands of real kids. And to the Creator of everything, may the words of these stories bring smiles to the faces of the children who will turn these pages.

Come visit me anytime, kids, on my Web site at http://www.beckyfreeman.com! I'd love to hear from you.

1

LIfE INtERRUptED

Joy Bigsley lay on her back in her bedroom, her blond head on a pillow. The bright winter sun spilled through the window and across Joy's cozy leggings. She absently twisted one of her long blond curls that spread out like spaghetti on the hot-pink carpeted floor behind her.

This was Joy's favorite position for chatting on the phone with her best friend, Maria Garcia.

"I just finished reading the best book last night!" Joy said. "It's called *The Matchmaker's Daughter*. It was about how in olden times, parents would go to the village matchmaker, who would help them pick out a husband for their daughters."

"Ugh," came Maria's voice over the receiver. "That sounds awful! Wouldn't you hate to have someone pick out who you were going to marry?"

"I know," said Joy. "What if they picked out a real nerd with a long warty nose who wore red socks and sandals?"

The two girls giggled, then Joy continued. "Well, in some countries back then, you just had to hope and pray the matchmaker would pick out someone you could love. In this book, the matchmaker's daughter was a beautiful teenager who had a kind heart. So she always tried to help her mother match up couples who really did love each other. It was *so* romantic."

Maria laughed. "Joy, that would have been a perfect job for you—matchmaking. Too bad it's gone out of style, huh?"

Joy agreed. "I know, I couldn't help thinking I'd be really good at this. Remember how I introduced Mr. Henley to Miss Nellie last spring? And you know the end of that happily-ever-after story."

Maria and Joy talked about the wedding between Mr. Henley, who owned the hardware store in Tall Pines, to Miss Nellie, who owned the café where they often went for ice cream after school. Mr. Henley and Miss Nellie had gotten married in the old cabin in the woods of Camp Wanna Banana, the Christian camp where Joy lived along with her twin brother, Jake, and her parents. Maria and her twin brother, Marco, also lived at Camp Wanna Banana with their parents. Mr. Garcia, Maria's father, helped Mr. Bigsley run the place.

Munch-Munch, Joy's pet spider monkey, sat at the foot of the bed while Joy chatted. The little monkey, hardly ever as quiet as she was today, was staring at a bright yellow book, patting the picture on the cover.

"That was the most beautiful wedding," Joy said. "And then they adopted all those great kids and—" Joy was interrupted by a beeping sound. "Wait a second, Maria," she told her friend. "Someone else is calling in."

She punched a button on the phone. "Hello?"

"Hey, Joy. How are ya?" came the voice of her Great-uncle Dan. Joy hadn't seen him in years, but he'd been calling a lot since his sister, Joy's Grandma Pearl, had become sick.

"I'm okay," she said. "How's Grandma today?"

Great-uncle Dan paused for a minute before

answering. "Joy, I really need to talk to your mom," he said. "Can you go get her for me?"

Something about the way he said it made Joy's stomach knot up, but she ignored the feeling and said, "Sure. Just a second." She punched the button again.

"Maria, I gotta go," she said. "Mom's got a call."

"Call me when she's done," Maria told her. "Mama's making tamales today, and you know that's an all-day ordeal. Before you go, how's your Grandma Pearl?"

"Not so good," said Joy with a sigh. "She's in a lot of pain, and Dad said she's probably not going to live much longer. Mom's getting ready to go see her this weekend. But I can't stand to think about it! It's my Great-uncle Dan calling for Mom, so he might have more news today."

"Well, let me know," said Maria. "Your grand-mother is so sweet."

Joy knew she had to let her great-uncle talk to her mom, even though she didn't want her girl-talk with Maria to end. Joy's friends and books were the two things that made her feel better when she got too sad about Grandma.

"Tell your mama to save me a tamale, okay, Maria? I like the sweet ones she made last week, the ones with raisins and brown sugar inside the corn-meal mush."

After a quick good-bye, Joy punched the button one more time and then carried the phone downstairs to the living room, her bare feet making light prints on the carpet as she walked. Her mother was sitting on the floor among a pile of papers, notebooks, scissors, and markers. She was leafing through a flowered hatbox of old photos.

"Hi, Joyshines!" she said as Joy came into the room.

"Mom, Great-uncle Dan's on the phone for you." Joy handed the phone to her mom and then went back up the stairs to get Munch-Munch. It was never a good idea to leave the pet monkey alone for long.

Munchy was still looking at the yellow book, but now she was jumping up and down and screeching with delight. Joy laughed. "What are you reading, Munchy?" She walked over to her furry friend.

"Oh, now I see why you like this book," Joy said. "That's *Curious George!* He's a sweet little monkey just like you, but he gets in all kinds of trouble because he's a little *too* curious."

Munchy looked up at Joy and bared a row of tiny teeth, as if she were grinning most mischievously. Joy smiled at the little rascal. Playing with Munchy was one other thing that nearly always made Joy feel happy on sad days.

Joy scooped up Munchy and the book. "Let's go downstairs with Mom. I'll read this story to you, but then I'm going to help Mom with her scrapbooks." Munchy chattered happily, her arms around Joy's neck, as they headed out of the bedroom.

But before Joy even reached her mother, she could hear that something was just not right. The knot in her stomach returned, and Munchy's happy chatter stopped. When Joy stepped into the living room, what she saw stopped her in her tracks. Her mother, still holding the phone, was resting her head on the coffee table, crying.

2

PRICELESS PEARL

"M om," Joy said gently, coming out of her shock. "What's wrong?" She walked over to the table and touched her mother's shoulder.

Joy's mom raised her head. She looked like a raccoon where she'd cried her mascara into dark rings under her eyes.

"Oh, Joyshines," she said, taking her daughter's hand and squeezing it affectionately. "Dan called to tell us that Grandma Pearl died in her sleep at the hospital this morning."

Joy felt as though something heavy and horrible

had landed in the middle of her stomach. She sank to the floor beside her mother, her legs suddenly jelly. They sat and hugged and cried together for a few minutes.

"I guess we all knew that this day would come, Joy," her mother said through tears. "Grandma has been in the hospital for so long with that awful cancer. Part of me is relieved that she's out of pain and with your Grandpa and Jesus. But there's another part of me that feels as small as the little girl in this picture."

She handed an old faded photo to Joy. It was Joy's mom as a little girl. She had deep dimples in her cheeks, her hair in two brown braids, and wore overalls and a pink T-shirt. She was sitting on a porch swing next to a smiling woman in a blue-checked apron, a young Grandma Pearl. They were shelling green peas into a big metal pan.

Mrs. Bigsley stared at the photo as she said, "I was just sorting through these old photos… Oh, Joy, I didn't know that at my age I could feel so much like a child who misses her mommy!"

Joy nodded in sympathy. "I miss her too, Mom."

"I know, baby." She sniffed as she gently stroked Joy's hair with the palm of her hand. "Joy, I will need to find your dad and Jake. I think they're over at the

Treetop Meeting House taking down the Christmas decorations. Will you be okay staying here in case your great-uncle calls again?"

"Okay," said Joy, leaning her head on her mother's shoulder. "Don't worry. I'll be fine."

But as soon as Joy's mother walked out the door, Joy thought of her Grandma Pearl—of her warm hugs that smelled lightly of Dove soap, her delicious home cooking, her beautiful garden, and her old, worn-out Bible. Joy didn't feel fine at all. She felt empty and unbelievably sad. As she climbed into her favorite reading chair by the window that overlooked Lake Willapango, she buried her face in one of the pillows and sobbed.

3

HEAVEN-SENT COOKIE?

A month had gone by since Grandma Pearl had gone to live in heaven, but to Joy sometimes it seemed as if it were only yesterday. Since her grandma had lived in Kentucky, Joy only saw her once or twice a year, but she and Joy had a special bond anyway. Even though everyone was happy that Grandma was with Jesus now, her absence left a big hole in Joy's heart.

"Remember Grandma Pearl's giant oatmeal raisin cookies?" Joy asked over dinner one night.

Mom smiled. "Nobody made any better cookies. Or any *bigger* ones. She baked them in a pizza pan!"

"And then she'd decorate it like a giant gingerbread man's head with curly icing hair and M&M eyes and a red licorice mouth!" Jake added, licking his lips.

"There will never be another Grandma Pearl," Dad said with sigh. He put his fork on his plate, finished with the hearty supper of pot roast and veggies. Grandma Pearl had been especially fond of Joy's dad; maybe, Joy always thought, because his parents had died before Jake and Joy were born.

"No, there won't," agreed Joy as she stood to clear the dishes.

The phone rang and Joy's mother reached for it. "Hello?... Yes, this is Mrs. Bigsley." She paused. "Uh-huh." Another pause. "Yes. Well, how nice of you. Why, that would be very special. Do you know how to get here?" Joy looked at her mom and mouthed, "Who is it?" Her mom held up a finger as if to say, "I'll tell you in a minute."

"Okay. I'll put the teakettle on, and we'll see you in a few minutes." Mom slowly put the phone on its base and looked at her family with a half-smile, a mixture of pleasure and confusion.

Joy picked up another blue-and-white plate and carried it to the kitchen. "Who was that?"

"It was a woman who called herself Mopsy," she answered almost dreamily.

"Mopsy?" Jake asked, just before gulping down a last bit of milk. "Sounds like a name for a rabbit."

Joy laughed. "Mopsy *was* one of Peter Rabbit's sisters in the Beatrix Potter story Grandma Pearl used to read to us when we were little."

Mrs. Bigsley acted as though she hadn't heard a word Jake and Joy said. Finally she blinked and said, "This Mopsy woman said she baked a huge oatmeal raisin cookie that she wanted to bring over to give to our family."

Jake gasped. "*Wow!* Do you think Grandma Pearl heard our dinner conversation and asked Jesus to tell the angels to figure out a way for us to have an oatmeal cookie tonight?"

Everyone laughed, except for Mom, who seemed to be slowly coming back to her old self from some dream world. She looked at Jake and said, "Son, nothing would surprise me about your Grandma Pearl. She's probably wearing out the angels telling them about her wonderful grandkids back on earth—just like she used to wear out the neighbors by showing them your school pictures every chance she got!"

Joy could just imagine her grandmother bragging on her and Jake all over heaven. *I guess most grandmothers think their grandkids are absolutely perfect,* she thought. *I'm going to miss having someone feel that way about me!*

A half-hour later, Jake and his dad were out in the garage getting their gear ready for a snowshoe trip they'd planned for the coming weekend. Joy had finished cleaning up the kitchen, and her mom had put the kettle on the stove for tea when they heard a knock at the front door.

4

HOT TEA AND MYSTERIES

Hello, Mrs., er, Mopsy?" Mrs. Bigsley said as she opened the front door. "Come on in."

"Well, hello, dear!" the silver-haired woman answered cheerfully. Joy came to stand beside her mother and took note of their visitor. She was a pretty, grandmotherly lady, her hair pulled up in a French twist. She was bundled in a waist-length winter jacket, her legs covered by a long denim skirt and red Roper boots. The smell of warm cookies drifted to Joy's nose from the giant, foil-covered cookie sheet Mopsy held.

"Come in, come in," Joy's mom said. "Let me help you with that pan!"

"I'll take your jacket," Joy offered politely.

"Why, thank you," Mopsy said. She unzipped it, revealing a red-and-yellow floral shirt with a small white bunny embroidered on the pocket.

Mopsy followed Joy and Mrs. Bigsley into the kitchen. "I suppose I should tell you my real name is Molly McBride. I was a first-grade teacher for years, and I always decorated my room with the characters from *Peter Rabbit*—my favorite book to read to the children on the first day of school. One year, after reading aloud about Flopsy, Mopsy, Cottontail, and Peter, one of the students got tongue-tied and called me 'Miss Mopsy' instead of Mrs. McBride. From that day forward I was known as Miss Mopsy, and then when I retired, my friends just started calling me Mopsy. My late husband shortened it even more—he often called me Mops."

Joy laughed and found herself already liking this new friend.

Jake rushed in from the garage, holding a snowshoe. "I smell cookies!" he said, immediately sighting the pan.

Mopsy looked at Jake, then Joy, approvingly. "So you must be the 'most wonderful grandchildren in the world.'"

Jake simply nodded. "Yep, that's us."

"Jake!" Joy said. "That sounds prideful."

He shrugged. "Well, that's what Grandma Pearl always called us."

Joy's mother lifted loose foil off the cookie sheet and drew in her breath as she stared at the giant, still-warm cookie. Jake shouted, "Cool!" and Joy said, "Wow!" It was decorated exactly like the head of a gingerbread man, in the very same way Grandma Pearl used to decorate her enormous oatmeal cookies.

At this, Mopsy stood up and took Mrs. Bigsley's hands.

"Dear, I have been a close friend of your mother's for some years. She told me many wonderful stories about you and the children and specifically asked me to look in on you when she was…gone. She told me that making this cookie for the most wonderful grandchildren in the world was a special tradition of hers. So, of course, I had to come see you. The folks at the bed-and-breakfast were kind enough to let me use their kitchen to make this."

Mrs. Bigsley's lips trembled a bit as she poured three cups of hot tea for "the girls" and handed Jake two cans of soda pop, one for him and one for Dad.

"I was terribly sad not to be able to attend her

funeral and meet you there," Mopsy continued, "but I was ill at the time and couldn't travel far from my doctor's care. But I am feeling fine now." She took a sip of her chamomile tea. "Mmm," she said. "Delicious."

Mrs. Bigsley cut the cookie into wedged-shaped pieces and put two in a napkin for Jake to carry out to the garage.

"Thanks!" hollered Jake as he headed out the kitchen door, barely managing with the snowshoe, cookies, and sodas. "It's nice to meet you, Mrs. Rabbit." The door shut behind him, and for a minute everything was absolutely quiet. Joy swallowed hard, completely embarrassed by Jake's mistake, but not quite knowing what to say to fix it.

Thankfully she didn't have to, because Jake soon reopened the door and said, "Oops, I meant Mrs. *Mopsy!*" Everyone laughed.

"Jake tries hard," explained Joy after swallowing a bit of cookie. "He's just a little bit odd. Sometimes he gets his words mixed up. Actually, sometimes I think Jake's whole brain is mixed up!"

"Joy!" said Mrs. Bigsley in mock shock.

"Well, Mom," Joy said, "he does wear upside-down buckets on his head sometimes."

"Well, yes, but…"

"And he does kiss frogs."

"Well, yes…"

Mopsy laughed out loud. "Sounds like Jake is quite unique. I had a few like him when I taught school. I never knew whether to hug them, laugh at them, or send them to the principal's office!"

Mrs. Bigsley sighed. "Yes, that's our Jake."

Joy's mother sat down at the table, lifted a cup of tea to her lips, took a slow sip, then set the delicate blue-and-white china cup into its saucer. "This was so kind of you, Mopsy, to come see us. We are doing a little bit better every day since Mother died. Some days I don't even cry at all. I'm so thankful for all the good memories we have of her." In spite of her happy talk, a tear fell down Mrs. Bigsley's cheek. "My mother was a remarkable lady."

Mopsy pulled her chair next to Joy's mother's and pulled her into a warm, comforting embrace. "I know, honey, I know." Joy couldn't help thinking how childlike her mother seemed right now, and how grateful she was that Mopsy had come out of nowhere to help comfort her mother. She imagined it was almost like getting a visit from an angel!

In a few moments tears were dried, and the three of them began talking and laughing over cookies and tea. Joy thought it strange that Mopsy wouldn't eat any of the cookie, saying that the tea was enough to satisfy her. It was another hour before Mopsy looked up at the clock and declared it was time for her to get to bed. Mrs. Bigsley and Joy felt as though they'd known Mopsy forever by the time they said their good-byes.

Joy looked in her mother's weary eyes after closing the front door behind Mopsy. "I'll clean up the kitchen, Mom."

"That would be so great, Joyshines," sighed her mother as she turned toward the living room to take the stairs up to her bedroom. "Thank you."

As Joy cleared the table once again, she noticed a lavender envelope on the floor, near the chair where Mopsy had been sitting.

I wonder what that is, she thought. The carefully handwritten envelope read, "Mrs. Molly McBride. Personal and Confidential."

This must have fallen out of Mopsy's purse, thought Joy as she held it in her hands. *I wonder what's inside?* "Personal and Confidential," she read again. Joy suddenly felt like Curious George. *I'll just take one little peek. What can it hurt?*

5

STRANGER WITH A PAST

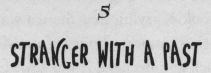

The pretty envelope had already been torn open, probably by Mopsy herself. Joy felt a bit like a spy as she pulled out the enclosed paper, but she was too curious to stop herself. *No one will know,* she thought. Joy carefully unfolded the pretty, flower-print paper and discovered a handwritten note to Molly from Pearl. Joy's Grandma Pearl!

My dear Molly,
Don't worry, your secret will die with me. No
one ever need know about the past. And you

know that I owe you more than words can say for what you did for us! God alone holds our future. I am enclosing a recent picture of the most wonderful grandchildren in the world.

I am sure you will agree when you meet them, after I am gone to be with my husband in heaven. How I will miss my darling family. But I cannot wait to see Jesus, and I feel it will be very soon now. I am tiring, as you can see by my wobbly writing.

God be with you as you look in on the children for me. Take care of yourself and watch that sugar tooth! Keep up your strength.

Love,
Pearl

What secret could Grandma and Mopsy be hiding? wondered Joy. *What did Mopsy do that could have been so awful that it had to be kept a secret? And what did Mopsy do for Grandma Pearl that was so wonderful it kept Grandma from revealing the secret?*

She thought of calling a meeting of the four amigos detectives to start an investigation. But something stopped her. What would Jake, Marco, and Maria think of her reading someone's private letter?

They might say she had made a bad choice. Had she? A guilty feeling crept into her stomach. But what if Mopsy was a criminal or something? Shouldn't Joy and her family know about it? She didn't want to get into an argument about that with her friends just then, so she decided not to call.

Now all Joy had were questions without answers—and doubt about whether she should even have those questions at all! She folded the letter and gently returned it to the envelope. She would need to give this back to Mopsy tomorrow.

FAMILY WARMTH

What would we have done without our Mopsy these past weeks?" Mrs. Bigsley asked between singing funny little ditties and putting ingredients for bread into a huge wooden bowl. Joy was helping her mom bake loaves of whole-wheat bread this Monday afternoon. She would take a loaf to Mopsy tomorrow after school. It had been three months since Mopsy entered the Bigsleys' home and steadily made her way into their hearts as well. Mopsy had lost her husband only the year before and had no other family back in Kentucky. With the Bigsleys'

encouragement, Mopsy bought a cute cottage just a mile down the road from Camp Wanna Banana and settled into a new life in Tall Pines.

Mopsy also began going to Pine Tree Chapel, the church the Bigsleys and Garcias attended. Yesterday, after Pastor Stevens's sermon on "Family Love," Joy overheard Mopsy talking to her mother as they visited on the front lawn. "I don't have a daughter to call my own, but if I did I'd have wanted her to be just like you, and I'd wish for grandchildren just like Jake and Joy." Her words were like the spring sun and filled Joy with warmth.

Though no one could take the place of Grandma Pearl in Joy's heart, Joy had to admit that Mopsy had become very much like another grandmother to her and Jake. Still, Joy hadn't forgotten the letter she found after their first meeting, and she often wondered what sort of secret Molly was hiding. Sometimes it made her feel suspicious, in spite of the affection growing between them. What if Molly was hiding a *dark* secret? But whatever was in Molly's past, Joy could not find anything mean-spirited about her now.

Joy was kneading the big bowl of dough when Jake burst through the back door, covered in mud from head to foot.

"Mmm," he said. The fragrant smell of yeast had filled the sunny yellow kitchen. "You're making homemade bread!"

"Jake Bigsley!" Mrs. Bigsley shouted, too over-whelmed at the sight of Jake to pay attention to any-thing he was saying. "What have you been doing?"

Jake gave a "What's the big deal?" shrug. "Marco and I wondered what it would be like to be pigs, so we took some buckets of lake water and made a big ol' mud pond and rolled around in it while we oinked and squealed."

He said this as though rolling around in mud and oinking were normal activities all boys do on a Mon-day afternoon. Then he paused and grinned, his white teeth gleaming from his mud-covered face. "Man, pigs have the *life!*"

Mrs. Bigsley raised one eyebrow and pointed to the door. "Outside, young man! To the water faucet. *Now!*"

Jake shrugged his muddy shoulders and reluctantly turned to go. Dark puddles dripped behind him as he walked across the clean kitchen floor. Mrs. Bigsley turned to Joy, sighed, and said, "Joy, honey, I love that crazy brother of yours, but have I told you lately how glad I am to be with an understanding daughter like you on days like this?"

A cozy "mom and me" feeling—a feeling sort of like friendship, only better—welled up in Joy's heart at her mother's comment, the way their wheat bread would soon rise in the warmth of the pan.

7

DIARY SECRETS

Joy parked her bicycle in front of Mopsy's charming blue cottage with white trim, then walked along the rose garden that would soon be bursting with velvety blossoms. Shifting her backpack so it was easier to carry, she continued up a rusty-red brick path and knocked on the door. Four little statues of pudgy rabbits sat on the porch by the door. The names "Flopsy," "Mopsy," "Cottontail," and "Peter" were engraved on their carved stone shirts. The Bigsleys had given them to Mrs. Molly "Mopsy" McBride last month on her birthday.

Mopsy opened the door, her blue-green eyes

dancing with delight. "Why, Joy! What a pleasure to see my favorite girl knocking at my door this fine morning. What have you got there?"

Joy reached into her backpack, pulled out a foil-wrapped loaf of wheat bread, and handed it to Mopsy.

Mopsy smiled, two dimples appearing on each side of her mouth, making her look much younger than her sixty years. "My favorite! Wheat bread! Your sweet mother knows this is one of the few treats I can still enjoy since the doctor made me stop eating sugar. This diabetes is the pits, let me tell you. I don't recommend it to anyone!"

Beckoning Joy inside, Mopsy caught sight of her rose garden. "Oh, my little buds look thirsty out there, don't they? Why don't you come on in the kitchen, Joy, and cut us two big slices of bread while I run out and water the roses real quick. There's some butter in the fridge and some cold milk for us to drink with it."

Joy's stomach growled as if in response. Laughing, she said, "I guess I am pretty hungry!"

Mopsy hugged Joy affectionately before heading out the door toward the water hose. Joy walked into the cottage and quickly found her way to the kitchen that had become familiar to her in the past several weeks. She set the bread down on the blue tile counter and turned to look for a bread knife. Her eye spotted a pink checked notebook lying nearby. The words "My Journal" were printed on the cover. *Maybe the answers to my questions about Mopsy are in there,* she thought, feeling strangely like Curious George again. She probably shouldn't peek, but who would know? No one had found out that she had read Mopsy's private letter. What could it hurt? Knowing she shouldn't peek but too curious to stop herself, Joy flipped through the handwritten pages to today's date: April 16.

Her eyes landed on a sentence, written in Mopsy's pretty script:

> My darling, if only I could tell you of my secret love. It pains me that I may not speak of this plainly, or tell you of how I've been praying for you, love you, and long to be near you.

Joy gasped. Mopsy was in love! But with whom? *How many secrets does this sweet, innocent-looking lady have?*

Joy heard the front door open and shut. She quickly closed the diary and began hunting for the knife again.

"How are you doing in there, Joy?" Mopsy asked as she walked down the hall.

"Um, I'm, um…*fine*," Joy finally sputtered.

"Good! I'm going to wash up and I'll be there in just a minute."

While Mopsy was washing her hands in the bathroom, Joy found the knife, cut two thick slices of soft brown bread, and laid them on a lemon-yellow plate. As she spread creamy butter over the soft slices, her mind whirled. *Poor Mopsy must be so lonely, living all alone after her husband died and with no children of her own. But now she's in love with a man, and she's afraid to tell him! Maybe she is so ashamed of whatever she did in the past that she's afraid another man won't love her!*

Joy poured two tall glasses of ice-cold milk and set them on the antique oak dining table. *Well, whatever Mopsy did, it couldn't be that bad. She's the nicest lady I've ever met, next to Grandma Pearl. She deserves to have a new husband if that's what she wants. And I'm just the one to help her out.*

Joy paused briefly from her work. *First, I just have to figure out who she loves so I can get them together.* She looked out the kitchen window at a red cardinal perched on a nearby tree limb. "Hey, pretty birdie," Joy said quietly, a slow smile spreading across her face. "I'm Joy Bigsley—but you can call me The Matchmaker."

8

PADDLEBOAT POW-WOW

"I have a mystery to solve!" Joy nearly shouted to Maria over the phone. "Can you and Marco meet Jake and me at the Treetop Meeting House in thirty minutes?" Even though she'd have to confess that she had virtually spied on Mopsy, Joy decided she had to have the help of the four amigos after all.

"Why not at the cabin in the woods?" asked Maria. "That's where the four of us usually meet for detective work."

"I know, but Dad's getting the cabin ready for summer camp now, turning it into a camp nature center and first-aid station again. He promises we can have it back for our clubhouse after the summer program at Camp Wanna Banana is over, but for now…"

"Okay! See you at the tree house in thirty minutes! Can you bring Munchy? I miss her!"

"Not today," Joy said. "Mom's taken her over to visit Mopsy. You know how she loves Munch-Munch. She sewed Munchy a new outfit for the Camp Wanna Banana fund-raiser and needs Munchy to try it on. She said she thought the mascot of the camp should look extra spiffy for the big day."

"She's such a nice lady," said Maria.

"I know," said Joy. "And she's part of the mystery."

Jake and Joy paddled their canoe along the grassy banks of Lake Willapango, the fastest route to the Treetop Meeting House. "What's that?" Joy asked, pointing to a large boxlike contraption near the shore. It was the color of a ripe banana.

"Didn't Maria tell you?" Jake asked, as he lifted up the brim of his cowboy hat. No matter how often Joy begged, Jake would not give up wearing crazy hats in public. She was just grateful that he didn't wear his huge Mexican sombrero today. Jake continued, "Dad and Mr. Garcia bought a paddleboat for Camp Wanna Banana yesterday. Looks like Marco and Maria are trying it out! They must have come across the lake from their house."

Marco and Maria waved from the shore under the shade of the Treetop Meeting House above them. "So how do you like *Monkey Business?*"

"What?" asked Joy, not understanding.

Maria laughed. "That's what your dad named the new paddleboat!"

Jake and Joy stepped out of the canoe, admiring the bright four-seater boat.

"Cooool!" said Jake, unable to contain his excitement over a new piece of play equipment. "Let's try it out!"

Joy shrugged. "I guess we could have our meeting on the paddleboat instead. Are there enough life jackets?"

Marco nodded, his straight black hair bouncing in the breeze. "Of course. Safety first, you know." Joy grinned. Marco had recently decided that he wanted to be a doctor when he grew up. He was taking a first-aid course after school so he could be a safety patrol helper at Camp Wanna Banana this summer.

Soon the foursome had their life jackets on and

paddled out toward the middle of the lake. The springtime sun made the day just right, Joy thought—not too hot and not too cold. It wasn't long before Jake and Marco peeled off their shirts and prepared to dive off the boat in their shorts.

"Hey, I need to tell you guys about my mystery!" Joy said, trying to stop them.

"Play first, work later," Jake said with a grin. "We've got time, Joy. C'mon!" He dove off the boat with Marco while Maria and Joy looked on and braced themselves for their brothers' splashes.

"These are times when I wish I were a boy," said Maria. "Next time, let's you and me wear our bathing suits and leave the guys at home."

Joy agreed.

"Forget about the guys," Maria said. "Tell me what's up. What's the new mystery?"

Joy explained what she'd discovered when she'd read Mopsy's letter and diary.

"Oooooh," said Maria, placing her hand on her chest. "A secret love! That is so romantic. But, Joy, you really shouldn't have read her personal stuff."

"I know," Joy agreed, lowering her eyes. "But I couldn't help myself."

Maria empathized. "I'm not sure I could have

kept from looking either. Still, God promises to help us do the right thing whenever we're tempted to do something wrong."

Joy wondered for a moment if she should confess more to Mopsy. But Maria interrupted her thoughts.

"Who do you think the mystery man is?"

"Well, I've been wondering about that too. Do you know any man in town, about Mopsy's age, who isn't married?"

"There's Joe Riley, the mailman."

Joy laughed. "There's a good reason Joe Riley isn't married."

"Red socks and sandals."

"You got it," said Joy. "And he still lives with his mother. I just don't think he's Mopsy's type."

Maria nodded, leaning back in the paddleboat seat. Suddenly she sat up straight and said, "I bet I know who it is!"

"Who?" asked Joy.

"Pastor Stevens from Pine Tree Chapel."

Joy wrinkled her brow as she thought it over. "You know, Maria, I think you might be right! He's been a widower for about four years now, and Mopsy is always smiling and taking notes on his sermons—even the boring ones."

"Wouldn't they be cute together?" Maria thought aloud.

"Adorable," agreed Joy. "Now all we have to do is get him to ask her out on a date."

"Hey, Joy," Maria interrupted, worry in her voice. "Where are the boys?"

Joy surveyed the water around them. There was no sign of Marco and Jake anywhere in the calm lake around them. But before she could yell for her brother, the two boys swam out from under the paddleboat and splashed their sisters until they were soaking wet.

That did it. Joy stood up and in a no-nonsense voice said, "Take off your shoes, Maria. They think because we're girls and we don't have our bathing suits on, we'll sit here like sissies and let them splash us. Well, forget *that*. We're going in after them!"

Maria grinned and kicked off her sandals. "That's what I like about you, Joy."

"What's that?"

"You are full of surprises, and you aren't afraid to dive into life!"

Joy looked over at Jake who was doing a back-stroke, his orange life vest keeping him afloat. He looked like the giant peach with skinny arms and legs from Fruit of the Loom TV commercials. "Well, to tell you the truth, I used to be a real wimpette. But with a brother like Jake, you either fight him or join him in adventure. At least you join him *sometimes*. You won't be finding me wallowing like a pig in a mud puddle anytime soon, but as for swimming in our playclothes—last one in is a rotten egg!"

And with that, the girls, in their T-shirts and shorts, did two cannonball dives—so high and so hard that Jake and Marco were left blinking at each other in complete and total admiration.

9

MISSION: LOVE CONNECTION

Joy closed her Bible and stood up to sing the closing praise song with the rest of the congregation. She was relieved that the pastor's sermon had been short and easy to understand today. He spoke from the book of Ephesians about families again. Today's sermon was about husbands loving their wives and wives respecting their husbands and kids obeying their parents and parents not exasperating their kids. (That last part was always Joy's favorite.)

"In other words," Pastor Stevens said as he wrapped up, "if we just treat each other the way Jesus treated men and women and children, the world would be a much happier place. Go home and love each other today! I no longer have my wife, and my kids are grown and on their own." At this point, Pastor Stevens paused for a second before he concluded, "Sometimes you don't know how much family means until they are gone."

Joy glanced over at Mopsy and couldn't help but notice a tear at the corner of her eye as she smiled sweetly at Pastor Stevens. It *had* to be him! He had to be the one Mopsy secretly loved. Now all Joy had to do was let Pastor Stevens know this, and two lonely people would find happiness again!

Joy waited in the back of the church until most of the Sunday morning crowd had left the sanctuary and gathered on the front lawn to chat about where to go out for lunch. Mustering all her courage for the sake of true love, Joy approached Pastor Stevens.

The pastor's kind brown eyes crinkled at the edges as he smiled down at her.

"Pastor," Joy began, swallowing hard, "do you ever get lonely?"

"Joy," he answered thoughtfully, "I suppose I do sometimes. But the church people here, well, they've become like a family to me. And that helps."

"But don't you ever wish you had someone, like a *lady* someone, to take out to Miss Nellie's Café? Or someone to take long walks with while the sun sets? Maybe even someone whose hand you could hold?"

Pastor Stevens chuckled. "Okay, Joy. What are you up to?"

"I'm just thinking that Mrs. McBride—we call her Mopsy—would make a nice hand-holder. That's all."

"Well, Joy," Pastor Stevens asked, "what makes you say that?"

Joy motioned for Pastor Stevens to lean down so she could whisper in his ear.

"She likes you. A lot. I know it for a *fact*."

When Pastor Stevens stood straight up again, he had a funny look in his eyes.

"Just think about it," Joy said. "Maybe you might even ask her on a date or something."

Pastor Stevens nodded absently. Then he shook his head, as if someone had poured a bucket of cold water on him, and cleared his throat.

"Well, thank you for sharing that with me, Joy. I think I see your parents looking for you outside there. And there's the Henley family; I need to see how the newlyweds and their adopted family are coming along!"

"Maybe you'll be the next newlywed," Joy said in

an almost whisper, before waving good-bye to Pastor Stevens with a smile. Her matchmaking operation was successfully underway!

"Jaaaaaake! Joy!"

Their mother's voice came up the stairs, and Jake nearly ran over Joy in a race to get down to breakfast first.

Though Joy was used to her brother's crazy outfits, she couldn't help noticing that Jake's light blond hair was an odd shade of purple this morning. She eyed it carefully before stepping into the kitchen and then said, "Nice color."

He grinned and said, "Thank you. It's Groovy Grape."

"Jake," Mrs. Bigsley said with a raised eyebrow, "did you put Kool-Aid in your hair again?"

Jake nodded.

His mother started to protest but stopped herself. Joy knew that her mother had decided to save her energy for more important things, since no matter what she did or said, Jake would always be a bit *different*.

"Mopsy called bright and early, sounding awfully happy," Mom said as she served up two plates of bacon, eggs, and wheat toast.

"Oh?" asked Joy with interest.

"Yes. She said she finished sewing Munchy's outfit, and it turned out adorable! Wait until you see the overalls, Joy. They're completely covered with shiny yellow sequins. And then she made her a hot-pink, blue, and yellow-striped shirt to go under it."

"That's nice," said Joy, trying not to sound disappointed. She'd hoped that Pastor Stevens might have paid Mopsy a visit yesterday after church. "Did she mention anything else?"

"Well, as a matter of fact she did. Said she received a big bouquet of flowers this morning from a secret admirer."

"Oh." Joy tried to look as though she were simply pondering.

Mrs. Bigsley sat down and took a sip of orange juice. "Joy, will you go over to Mopsy's this afternoon after school and pick up Munchy's outfit for me?"

"Sure," said Joy, feeling rather proud of herself. She was sure it wouldn't be long now before Mopsy became a "Mrs." Perhaps Joy would get to be her flower girl! It was all coming together so well. Just like a romantic movie, starring Joy Bigsley as the world's best matchmaker.

10

A BOUQUET OF SURPRISES

Joy could hardly wait until school was out so she could get over to Mopsy's. Maria, Marco, and Jake were going to come over to the cottage a little later, after finishing up their chores. Mopsy had promised to teach the four kids how to play Chinese checkers this afternoon. Mopsy and the two sets of twins enjoyed playing many a game of spades and spoons together after school. She really was an ideal grandmother type. Joy was sincerely sad that Mopsy had never had a child or real grandchild of her own.

"Come in, hon!" Mopsy said as soon as she opened the door for Joy. "Look at these beautiful flowers delivered from Miss Nellie's this morning. Did you know Miss Nellie has expanded her café into a gift and floral shop?" Joy admired the spring bouquet of daisies, tulips, miniature roses, and baby's breath.

"Oh yeah," Joy answered. "I heard that! These are beautiful! Do you know who sent them?"

"Yes, I do," Mopsy said, looking both pleased and puzzled. "Pastor Stevens called this afternoon and confessed he sent the flowers. Then he asked me to an outdoor concert next Saturday night. Wasn't that a sweet invitation? It's so unexpected."

Joy smiled. "But don't you have sort of a, well, a crush on Pastor Stevens?"

"What?" Mopsy asked, obviously shocked. "Why in the world would you think that, child? I am happy as I can be right now. Now, I love Pastor Stevens as a friend and a spiritual leader. But I don't want to date anyone or get married again." Mopsy pointed to a portrait of her husband and herself, taken on their fortieth anniversary. "No, Joy, one good long marriage to one wonderful husband is enough for me. I miss him every day, but I'm starting to have lots of fun again."

Joy's stomach did a quiet flip-flop. But then... who was Mopsy's secret love? If she outright asked her that question, Mopsy would find out that Joy had read her diary. She couldn't tell her *that!*

"So what did you say?" Joy asked.

"Well, I don't see any harm in a good concert, dear. That's one of those fun things I can simply enjoy doing with a friend. After all, it's not like he suggested we start courting!"

Joy smiled nervously.

Mopsy was still talking. "There are some great things about living alone. I can do anything I want to do anytime I want to do it—eat pancakes for supper, make a big mess of sequins and monkey costumes in the middle of the house, go off on a trip to Italy to paint in watercolors. I'm having a ball just being with myself and my Lord, who takes such good care of me. God is like a friend who never leaves my side."

Poor Pastor Stevens would be so confused and hurt when he found out that Joy had been mistaken! *What a mess I am in,* thought Joy. *What now?*

She was saved from having to say anything by a knock at the door, followed by the voices of Jake, Marco, and Maria.

"Come on in!" Joy called.

"I'd better pull out the snacks," Mopsy said with a smile, disappearing into the kitchen. Jake and Marco followed her, leaving Maria and Joy alone with the flowers.

"So were these from Pastor Stevens?" Maria whispered. Joy had told her best friend the latest news during lunch at school.

Joy nodded that they were. "But, Maria," she said, "I think I've made a really big mist—"

"Joy!" Jake ran out of the kitchen, his eyes wide with fear. "Joy, come quick! Maria, call 911! Mopsy's lying on the floor, not moving!"

11

EMERGENCY!

The three dashed back into the kitchen, and Maria grabbed the phone off the wall near the refrigerator. Marco was sitting on the kitchen floor with Mopsy's head in his lap.

"Mopsy!" he was saying, as he gently raised her head. "Can you hear me? It's Marco. Mopsy?"

Mopsy moaned a little bit. Joy heard Maria giving the emergency staff Mopsy's address and thought her beating heart might burst through her chest. "Marco, is she going to be all right?"

Maria interrupted them. "Marco, they want to

know if she's breathing." He nodded, and Maria relayed the information.

"Does she have a pulse?" Maria asked.

Marco put his hand to Mopsy's wrist to feel her pulse, just as he had been taught in first-aid class. "She does, but it's weak." He noticed a silver bracelet around her left wrist. "Hey, a medical bracelet," he said, turning it over to read. "Says she's diabetic."

"She is," Joy confirmed. "She's mentioned it before."

Maria told the person on the phone and paused to listen.

"They say it might be insulin shock," Maria said seriously. "We should try to get her to drink some orange juice."

"What's insulin shock?" Joy asked as Jake ran to the refrigerator and poured some juice in a small glass and gave it to Marco.

"Mrs. McBride?" He held it up to her lips. "Mopsy? Can you take a sip of this juice?"

Mopsy mumbled something and took a few sips of the juice before passing out again.

"The ambulance is on its way," Maria said quietly, still holding the phone.

All they could do was wait.

The Bigsleys and the Garcias, along with Pastor Stevens, sat in the waiting room of the hospital.

The cold, tiled halls seemed unfriendly and frightening, Joy thought. *Dear Lord,* she prayed silently. *Please, please don't take Mopsy home yet. We need her down here. And, Lord, I'm sorry for looking in Mopsy's diary and reading that note. I've really messed things up. Please don't take Mopsy away!*

Mopsy's friends had already been there for two hours. Sometimes they would pray, sometimes they would pace. It seemed to Joy as though the world had come to a standstill. How much longer would it take for the doctors to find out whether Mopsy would be okay?

Señora Garcia had her arm around Mrs. Bigsley, comforting her in her soft Spanish accent. "My friend, I am so sorry. I know how you love Señora Mopsy."

Joy thought her heart would break. Even Pastor Stevens seemed emotional. "I keep thinking what a fool I've been," he confessed to his friends gathered near. "I think I've loved Molly McBride since the first day she walked into church and gave me a little stuffed rabbit as an early Easter present." Joy slumped in her hospital chair. She did not have the heart to tell

Pastor Stevens that she'd made a terrible mistake, that Mopsy didn't want to date him or anyone.

Pastor Stevens continued. "She told me the rabbit was to remind me that people are a little like Peter Rabbit, who was a little like the Peter of the Bible."

"I never thought of that," Jake said. "I guess both Peters messed up a lot, but they had good hearts."

"That's right," said Pastor Stevens. "Peter Rabbit disobeyed his mother and went into Mr. MacGregor's garden—and ended up sick! Peter of the Bible promised to always be Jesus' friend, then later, he told someone he didn't even know Jesus! And he was sick at heart about it. But Peter's mother forgave her son, and Jesus forgave Peter."

Pastor Stevens paused for a moment and then said, "Molly told me, 'Pastor Stevens, sometimes we do good, and sometimes we do bad. Sometimes we feel sick when we realize we've done something wrong. But God loves us all the time, no matter what.'"

Joy closed her eyes and sighed. If only Mopsy knew how comforting those words were to her right now. God must have known Joy needed to understand that God's love was lots bigger than her messes and mistakes.

There was a rustle of starched cotton uniform as

two metal doors opened and a doctor walked through. "I'm sure you'll be glad to know Mrs. McBride is stabilized," he told them.

Everyone breathed one huge sigh of relief.

"However," the doctor said, "not only did we almost lose her to insulin shock, but her kidneys are failing. We have put her on dialysis—a machine that will cleanse her blood and do the work of healthy kidneys for her for the time being. But what Mrs. McBride really needs is a kidney transplant."

"Can we get that kind of plant down at the nursery?" Jake asked. Joy rolled her eyes.

The doctor explained that Mopsy needed a new kidney to live and that if they could find someone, usually a close relative whose kidneys matched the type Mopsy had, the relative could have an operation and give one of the kidneys to Mopsy.

"But what about the person who gives away their kidney?" asked Joy. "Won't they get sick and die?"

Marco answered, "No, Joy. God gives us two kidneys. But a person can live a long healthy life with just one."

The doctor nodded. "That's correct. Now, what we need to do is find Mrs. McBride's son or daughter or sister or brother—someone who might be a donor."

Mrs. Bigsley shook her head slowly. "Doctor, she has no living relatives."

The doctor drew in a long breath of deep concern. "Well, that will make our job more difficult. Not completely impossible but certainly more difficult."

12

HOPE IN A BOX

oy and Maria tiptoed into Mopsy's hospital room the next morning. She looked weak and pale.

"Hi, Mopsy," the girls said softly, as they touched her wrinkled hands.

Mopsy nodded in greeting, nearly too weak to talk.

"Mopsy," Joy said, "the doctor says you need a kidney. I wish I were your granddaughter so I could give you mine!" She thought she saw tears form in the corners of Mopsy's eyes.

"Mopsy," Joy said again, struggling to say what

53

she knew she must. "I have to tell you something. You know how Peter Rabbit sneaked into Mr. MacGregor's garden when he wasn't supposed to and ended up getting in all kinds of trouble? Well, I sneaked into your garden...sort of."

Mopsy's eyebrows wrinkled in question.

"I read the note to you from Grandma Pearl. The one that accidentally fell out of your purse at our house. And I read a part of your diary—the part about how you loved a certain someone but couldn't tell him that you loved him. I thought it was Pastor Stevens and I told him you loved him and then he sent the flowers to you and now he is waiting out there in the hall and he's going to come in to see you and he thinks..."

"That I am in love with him?" Mopsy whispered, raising her eyebrows. But her expression was soft, and she saw the worry on Joy's face. "It's all right, Joy. I forgive you," she said, patting Joy's hand.

Then using all the strength she had left, she whispered slowly, "There *is* a secret, Joy. And it looks like the time has come for me to tell it."

A nurse walked into the room and interrupted them. "I'm sorry, girls," she said, "but time's up." The nurse checked Mopsy's IV and adjusted a knob.

"This will put Mrs. McBride right to sleep so she can get some more rest."

Maria and Joy nodded and turned to leave, but not before they heard Mopsy say, "Secret...hope chest...look...find..."

"What?" asked Joy.

"Can you say that again, Mopsy?" asked Maria.

But Mopsy had closed her eyes and drifted into a deep sleep.

The sun seemed especially bright as Maria and Joy walked out of the hospital and waited for Mrs. Bigsley to pick them up. The red minivan soon came into view, and the girls hopped into the backseat.

"How's our Mopsy?" Joy's mom asked. "And how are my girls?" She smiled, and Joy couldn't help wishing that she'd inherited her mother's pretty dimples.

"She's weak," Joy answered.

Mrs. Bigsley nodded as she drove toward home. Joy looked out the window, noticing that they were near Mopsy's cottage. "Mom, could we stop by Mopsy's for a minute? I think she wanted us to look for something in—what was that thing she mentioned, Maria?"

"I think she wants us to look for something in a

hope chest," Maria answered. "What's a hope chest, Mrs. Bigsley?"

"A hope chest is a big wooden box with a hinged lid. Many are made out of cedar, and women store special things they want to save or keep in it," answered Mrs. Bigsley as she steered the car in front of Mopsy's house. "It's a tradition in some families that a young woman gets a hope chest when she turns sixteen, and she saves things in it that she'll use to make a home someday. Or sometimes she'll just store keepsakes and sentimental treasures."

Mrs. Bigsley slowed the minivan to a stop. "Girls, I'm going to give you the keys to the house and let you see if you can find her hope chest. Would you water the roses too? I'm going to run to the store for some milk and juice, and I'll come back to pick you up in about a half-hour."

The girls agreed, waved good-bye to Joy's mom, and entered the empty cottage.

"Even Flopsy, Mopsy, Cottontail, and Peter look sad and lonely," said Joy as she passed the four little statues.

"I know," answered Maria.

"Where do you think she'd keep a hope chest?" asked Joy.

"Maybe her bedroom?"

The girls walked down the hall to Mopsy's bedroom. The beautiful room was decorated with flower prints, antiques, and lace.

"I don't see anything that looks like a wooden box," said Joy.

"Wait," said Maria, walking to a corner in the room and lifting a homemade quilt that was draped over something. "I think I found it!"

"It's beautiful," said Joy as she removed the quilt and knelt to lift the reddish-brown lid. "It smells so good, like the cedar chips we put in Munchy's cage sometimes."

"What's inside?" asked Maria.

Joy lifted the lid and looked in. The chest was filled to the top with colorful, plush toy rabbits in all sorts of shapes and sizes.

"This must be her Peter Rabbit collection," Joy said.

"Oh yes!" said Maria. "She told me she buys them and saves them to give away as gifts."

"I don't get it," said Joy, scratching her head. "What's the big secret?"

"I don't know," said Maria, equally stumped.

Sadly, Joy said, "Then we are no closer to solving the mystery."

"What does it matter anyway?" asked Maria. "If Mopsy doesn't get a new kidney, how is some old secret going to help?

Joy nodded in agreement. "I know. I thought of that too. But there's something Mopsy wants us to know. And I want to try to figure it out."

"Maybe these rabbits aren't the actual secret," offered Maria, "but maybe they are a clue!"

"Yes!" said Joy. "Now you're thinking like a detective. Let's call an emergency meeting of the four amigos."

"Where?" asked Maria.

"Here, at Mopsy's house."

Thirty minutes later, Mrs. Bigsley honked, and the girls ran out to meet her.

"Mom, can we stay a little longer?" Joy asked. "We haven't watered the roses yet and we found the hope chest, but all it had in it was a bunch of stuffed rabbits."

"That's odd," said Mrs. Bigsley. "I wonder why a bunch of stuffed animals would be so important to Mopsy?"

"We don't know either," Joy answered. "But, Mom,

could you ask Jake and Marco to ride their bikes over here? We want to clean up the place real nice for Mopsy and could use their help. And maybe they can help us figure out the mystery too."

"Okay, girls, I'll tell them. And I'll drive the camp pickup truck by here before dark to pick up the four of you along with the boys' bicycles. Call me if you need me before then."

The girls nodded and turned back toward Mopsy's cottage as Mrs. Bigsley drove away.

Not long afterward, Joy saw Jake and Marco ride up to Mopsy's front door.

"Where are you?" the boys hollered as they opened the front door and walked in.

"Back in Mopsy's bedroom!" the girls shouted back.

Jake and Marco raced back to the bedroom, knocking each other down as they entered.

"Jake, don't goof off," Joy scolded. "We need you and Marco to help us solve a mystery."

At that, the boys stopped acting like playful puppies and stood at attention like two serious guard dogs.

"That's better," said Maria. Joy told the boys about Mopsy's letter and the diary entry she had read.

"That was really bad of you!" said Jake.

"Terrible!" said Marco.

Then almost at the same time both boys asked, "What did they say?"

Joy turned to Maria and said, "*See?* It's hard not to be curious!"

"Well? What did the letter and diary say?" Jake asked.

Joy explained everything: the letter, the diary entry, the misunderstanding with Pastor Stevens, and Mopsy's words to Joy at the hospital.

"But there was nothing in the hope chest but a bunch of fluffy stuffed bunnies!"

Marco rubbed his chin with his thumb. "Well, let's take another look at those rabbits."

The four amigos sat around the pile of stuffed animals, picking them up and examining each one. Jake suddenly asked, "What's that?"

"What?" asked Joy.

Jake pointed to the plush rabbit he held in his hands.

"That thing around this rabbit's neck."

Joy reached for the stuffed bunny. It was dressed in a little jacket and shorts, and a wooden carrot hung by a chain around its neck. Joy turned the carrot over and saw a hinge on one side. Was it the hinge to a door of some kind? Her thumbnail just fit into a crack opposite the hinge. She applied just a small amount of pressure, and it popped open, revealing a small compartment. She gasped. "Hey, there's a key inside this carrot! And there's a label on it too."

"What does it say?" asked Maria, leaning in for a closer look.

"Something…hope chest," Joy mumbled. "Wait, it has dust on it. Let me wipe it off… Okay, it says, *Key to hope chest.*"

"But Mopsy's hope chest doesn't have a keyhole," argued Maria. "And we've already opened it."

"Well then, that leaves only one option," Marco declared. "There must be another hope chest."

13

MYSTERY PHOTOS

W here do most girls keep hope chests?" asked Marco. "Come on, you two read all kinds of books about secrets and treasures and girl stuff. You must have an idea."

Joy and Maria looked at each other and immediately said, "The attic!"

"Does Mopsy even have an attic?" Jake asked.

"There's only one way to find out," answered Marco, already making his way down the hall, looking up at the ceiling. "Bingo! Here's the attic rope."

He yanked on it, and a creaky set of stairs unfolded as if from out of nowhere.

"Got your backpack?" Marco asked in Jake's direction.

"I'm way ahead of you," answered Jake as he reached in his pack. "Here's a flashlight."

Marco took the flashlight and led the four of them up into the darkness. Then he shone the light around until it landed on a small cedar chest, about the size of a computer monitor, sitting beneath a small arched window.

"Bingo again!" said Jake, moving in for a closer look. "This one has a keyhole in the lid."

"This hope chest looks small enough to bring downstairs," said Joy. "Let's take it down to the living room where there's more light."

A small furry creature ran across the room. Maria screamed. Then Joy screamed because Maria screamed.

"More light and less *mice!*" Maria shrieked.

Soon the four amigos were sitting cross-legged on the living room floor, staring at the box.

"Well, open it," Jake said to Joy, who was holding the key in her hand.

"I'm afraid to," said Joy. "What if there's a mouse in it?"

Marco laughed, and reached over to take the key from Joy. He put it in the keyhole, lifted the lid, and yelled, *"Mice!"*

The girls jumped and scrambled up on the couch. Marco and Jake doubled over laughing.

"Gotcha!" said Marco.

"Very funny," Maria said, her hand on one hip, her dark hair swinging behind her.

Joy and Maria climbed off the couch, ignoring the guys, who were still laughing. Looking into the open box, Joy saw nothing but a stack of yellowish papers.

Lying near the top was a big brown envelope, faded with age. Joy could make out the faint lettering on the outside of the envelope: "Age 1-6."

Curious, Joy opened the envelope and pulled out six smaller envelopes numbered one through six. She opened the first one and found pictures of a baby girl with light brown hair, learning to walk.

"Oh, how cute!" exclaimed Maria. "I wonder who she is?"

Joy shook her head. "I don't know. Mopsy said she never had any children of her own. Maybe she's a niece or something."

Joy continued to open the envelopes. Envelope number two held pictures from a birthday party of the same little girl blowing out two candles on a pink cake. Envelope number three held pictures of the girl on her third birthday, as did the others for each year. Joy opened the sixth envelope and gasped.

"What is it, Joy?" asked Marco.

Joy kept staring at the picture as she held it out for her friends to see. It was a faded photo of a little girl with deep dimples and long brown braids, dressed in a pink T-shirt and overalls, sitting on a porch swing, and shelling peas.

Her eyes wide, she spoke slowly. "This is Mom. These are all pictures of Mom. What does this mean?"

14

LOVE-LETTER CLUE

Joy and Maria looked up from the picture when they heard the front door open. Mrs. Bigsley's voice came through the entryway. "Are you ready to go yet, kids?"

"We're in the living room!" shouted Maria.

Mrs. Bigsley entered the room and looked at the girls' puzzled faces.

"Mom," asked Joy, "did you know Mopsy when you were a little girl?"

"Why, no," Mrs. Bigsley said. "We all met her at

the same time, remember—that night she brought the big cookie to our house. Why do you ask?"

"Because," said Joy as she handed the picture to her mother, "I was wondering why Mopsy has a picture of you when you were a little girl."

Mrs. Bigsley examined the picture. "Oh, my. Oh, my. This is really strange."

"I know," Joy agreed, "we have one almost exactly like it in our family album, only Grandma Pearl is sitting next to you."

"That's right," said Joy's mom. "Are there any other pictures?"

Joy handed her mom the pile. Mrs. Bigsley sank to the floor beside the girls as she looked through the stack.

"This is the weirdest thing," she said, looking at Joy. "These *are* all pictures of me—from each year of my life until I was six years old. What could this mean? If Mopsy knew me when I was a little girl, why didn't she say so? I'm so confused!"

"That makes three of us," Joy answered.

"Wait a minute," Maria said as she stuck her hand back into the largest envelope. "There is something down here." Maria pulled it out and looked at the envelope. "It's a letter." She handed it to Joy.

It was addressed to "My Darling Daughter."

Mrs. Bigsley took the envelope in her hands, which were shaking at this point, pulled out a thin piece of parchment paper, and read.

Darling Daughter of Mine,

If you are reading this letter, I will be nearing the end of my life or perhaps already in heaven.

Where do I begin? How can I explain?

When I was a young wife, I gave birth to a beautiful baby girl with dimples and lovely brown hair and eyes like a baby fawn's. You were perfect in every way. But you had arrived during our darkest days.

I was ill, too ill to take care of myself, much less a precious baby. And we were so poor we could hardly feed ourselves. We were in a desperate situation with no one to turn to, no one to help us, and no strength or money to carry us through. The doctor who delivered you sat down beside my hospital bed three days after you were born.

"Molly," he said, "you know that you have cancer. It is a miracle that you survived the birth of this child and that your baby survived as well!

You have no insurance to pay for your care. You need special treatments and around-the-clock care if you want to live. These treatments might take months, even years. The treatments are expensive, and we'll lower the charges as much as we can. But it's going to be all your husband can do to take care of you and pay the medical bills."

I didn't want to hear what the doctor said next, but I knew I had to, for your sake, my darling.

"Molly," he said, "I know a young couple here in town, Bob and Pearl, who are healthy and strong with plenty of money, a huge farmhouse, and two hearts overflowing with love. They want a baby more than anything but cannot have one of their own. They can care for your baby in ways that you simply cannot right now. Please consider—for your sake and your husband's sake and most of all for your baby girl's sake—letting Bob and Pearl adopt your baby. She will be loved and cared for, and you can focus on getting well again."

Your father and I both cried many tears over this, but we knew we had no other choice. We held you and kissed your sweet pink cheeks for the very last time. My heart broke that day, but in time, I did get my strength back, and eventually I overcame cancer. My husband and I enjoyed many more loving years together, although the cancer treatments left me unable to have more children.

Bob and Pearl cherished and cared for you. I asked them not to tell you that you were adopted and to always treat you as their very own. But I did ask them to please send me pictures of you each year.

I saved and kissed the pictures when they arrived, so happy that you were growing up beautifully. I thanked God every day for Bob and Pearl's love for you. She led you to Jesus when you were just five and she wrote a note to tell me so, knowing that I was a Christian too.

After your sixth birthday, the pictures didn't come as often. I thought perhaps your family had moved. I suppose, in a way, since I knew you were in wonderful hands, that it was easier to let you go as time went on. I trusted God with your life and tried to go on with my own. I earned a teaching certificate and taught first grade for twenty years, loving many children as I'd longed to love you, my daughter.

When your birth father died, I felt all alone in the world. But many years later Pearl found me to tell me she had cancer. We wrote to each other often then, and I think we became true friends through our mutual love for you, our daughter. When I had cancer, she mothered you. Now that she had cancer, she asked me to mother you in her absence. Of course, I was delighted. When Pearl went to be with the Lord, I wanted nothing more than to be close to you.

So I came to Tall Pines. And I discovered that you had grown into the sweetest woman imaginable with a joyful spirit, a song in her heart, God's love to share, and my dimples. (I cannot help being proud that I left two happy little marks on you!) Not only that, but you have two beautiful children, my grandchildren, Jake and Joy.

I have been so happy here, near you and the kids. I want you to know that I have never stopped loving you, not for a minute, since the day you were born. I have never stopped praying for you.

I hope you can find it in your heart to forgive me and Pearl for keeping this secret from you all these years. We kept it because we wanted you to

have a perfect childhood free of worry and concern. Perhaps we should have told you the truth
before now. If we made the wrong decision,
know we only wanted to do what we thought
was best for you.

Please know you never lost a mother and
father. You just had two sets of parents: One set
gave you birth and loved and prayed for you
daily; the other set raised you and loved and
prayed for you daily.

You were given a double portion of love!
Love,
Mopsy, Your "Other Mother"

Mrs. Bigsley sat without speaking for several minutes, just staring and thinking. She looked as if she
wanted to cry, but no tears fell. Marco and Maria
looked on in sympathy, while Jake and Joy sat beside
their mother, each one patting her back in comfort.

Then, after a bit, Mrs. Bigsley stood up and said,
"Come on kids, I'll sort out all these mixed-up feel-
ings another time. There's no time to waste right
now. I've got to see if I can save my mother's life
before I lose her again."

15

TWO MATCHES MADE IN HEAVEN

"Mom!" Joy whispered into her mother's ear. Mrs. Bigsley fluttered her eyes awake and moaned a little before saying, "Good morning, Joyshines. Is it all over?"

Before Joy could answer, Mr. Bigsley leaned down and kissed Joy's mother on the forehead. "I'm so proud of you. The operation went beautifully."

Mrs. Bigsley glanced around the room as best she could without lifting her head. "And Mopsy? Is she all right?"

"Mopsy's just fine!" Joy said as she patted her mother's arm.

Pastor Stevens, who'd been standing quietly nearby, cleared his throat. "Thanks to you, that is, Mrs. Bigsley. In fact, she's right here next to you."

"Mother?" Mrs. Bigsley asked, reaching out her hand.

"I'm here, darling," Mopsy answered groggily, reaching out to touch the hand of her daughter. "And I hope to be here for a long, long time."

Just then a surgeon walked into the room and said, "Ladies, this was one of the smoothest kidney transplants I've ever done. You two must have been a match made in heaven."

And with those words, Joy couldn't help but believe that Jesus and Grandma Pearl were looking down from heaven and smiling. Perhaps they were the real matchmakers in this story.

The two women lay next to each other holding hands, surrounded by their family and a love they could not see but everyone could feel.

Six months later, Mopsy looked as energetic and lovely as ever in her new Sunday dress in autumn colors of gold, red, and purple. Pastor Stevens cleared his throat from the pulpit and fixed his brown eyes on his parishioners.

"Welcome, everyone! I have great news to share," he said. "God answered our prayers for Mrs. Bigsley and Mrs. McBride. They are both in excellent health and feisty as ever. In fact, they are going to sing a duet this morning called 'I Come from a Long Line of Love.'"

There was a happy sigh from the congregation, who by now, knew their story well. Joy beamed. She'd almost made a real mess of things. She never should have read Mopsy's diary. She shouldn't have told Pastor Stevens about what she'd read. She knew that now. She let her curiosity get the best of her, and she was truly sorry.

That is why she was so surprised this Sunday morning. Because God, in His grace and mercy, not only forgave her, but He poured out His blessings in spite of her goof-ups. Mopsy was well, and Joy and her family were the happiest people in Tall Pines.

Well, almost the happiest people in Tall Pines.

Joy was thrilled when she learned that Pastor Stevens had won over Mrs. Mopsy McBride's heart, even after Joy had to tell him the truth about her mistake soon after Mopsy entered the hospital.

Though Pastor Stevens knew Mopsy loved him only as a good friend, he stayed by her side and helped nurse her back to health after the kidney transplant. One day, when Joy came to visit, Mopsy lay in her bed and said, "Joy, that nice Pastor Stevens has brought me supper every night since I've been home from the hospital. I just got my first look at myself in a mirror today and I'll tell you something—I look like something the cat dragged in. If Pastor Stevens can love me looking like this, I do believe he'd make an awfully good husband for somebody someday."

"Somebody?" Joy had asked, with a smile.

Mopsy nodded and winked. "Yes, just somebody. Someday."

To no one's surprise, Mopsy and Pastor Stevens had started officially dating during the summer at the Camp Wanna Banana fund-raiser, a big picnic given by the church to help send needy kids to camp. Joy heard that Pastor Stevens paid fifty dollars—the highest price ever bid—for Mopsy's boxed lunch and declared it to be the best bargain he ever struck since he got Mopsy's charming company to go with it. (He got Munch-Munch's company, too. The monkey was so pleased with her new outfit that she followed Mopsy everywhere that day!)

Mopsy, who truly thought she was too old "for such nonsense," finally admitted to the Bigsleys that even she was surprised to find out that "gray-headed grannies like me can really fall in love—like teenagers!—again."

As Joy listened to Mopsy and her mother harmonizing like angels from the pulpit, and as she watched Pastor Stevens, who was smiling like a junior-high kid, she said a silent "thank you" to the Matchmaker of heaven and earth.

THE TWIBLINGS' ACTIVITY PAGES

*Always ask an adult to help you
with these crafts and recipes!*

"GOD THINGS" DIARY

Turn a plain spiral notebook into a special diary. On the cover of the notebook, write your name and the words *God Things*. On the first page of your diary write the following verse: "Every good gift and every perfect gift is from above, and comes down from the Father" (James 1:17, NKJV).

Every day, write something good that God has given you to be happy about.

For example, you could write, *A friend at school asked me to sit by her* or *Today we got chocolate cake at lunch!* Maybe you read a special Bible verse that you liked—write it down. List all the good things that happened to you and say, "Thank you" to the Father above who sent them all your way!

JOY'S GIVING BREAD

Ask your parent to buy white or whole-wheat frozen bread-dough rolls in the freezer section of the grocery store. Let the rolls thaw and rise until you can handle and mold them. Wash your hands and put a little flour or butter on them to keep the dough from sticking to your fingers.

Make animals and people out of the dough. Try making fish, a rabbit, a turtle, a pig, or a monkey! Place them on a greased cookie sheet. Then brush your creatures with a little melted butter and bake at 325 degrees until they are golden brown. Put them on a paper plate, cover with foil to keep them warm and fresh, and take them to a neighbor for a special treat.

You'll need an empty glass or plastic container with a wide mouth and a screw-top lid. Decorate the container with markers, Con-Tact paper, or stickers.

Write the following phrases, adapted from the Bible's "Love Chapter," 1 Corinthians 13, on small pieces of paper. Fold them up. Each day, take one slip of paper out of the jar, read it, and ask God to help you to love your family and friends this way on this particular day.

- Love is patient.
- Love is kind.
- Love is not jealous.
- Love is not boastful or proud.
- Love is not selfish.
- Love is not rude.
- Love doesn't demand its own way.
- Love is not irritable or touchy.
- Love doesn't hold grudges.

- Love hardly notices when others mess up.
- Love is never glad about what is not true.
- Love is happy when the truth is told.
- Love is loyal, no matter what.
- Love believes.
- Love expects the best in others.
- Love defends its friends.
- Love is the greatest gift of all.

MUNCHY'S NEW CLOTHES

Mopsy made Munchy a new outfit! Can you help decorate it with crayons or markers? You can also glue on tiny buttons, sequins, or small scraps of material if you like.

CAMP WANNA BANANA
MATCH GAME

Using index cards, make matching pairs of cards with the names (or draw pictures) of the following people, places, or things from the Camp Wanna Banana Mysteries. Mix up the cards and lay them face down on the floor. Turn up two cards at a time, trying to find matching pairs. If you don't find a match, it's the next person's turn. The winner is the one with the most pairs of cards when all the cards have been matched up.

Jake
Joy
Marco
Maria
Munch-Munch
Banana Bash Zone
Cabin in the Woods
Treetop Meeting House

Mr. Bigsley
Mrs. Bigsley
Señora Garcia
Pastor Stevens
Mopsy McBride
Peter Rabbit
Hope Chest

GRANDMA PEARL'S
GIANT GINGERBREAD HEAD

You'll need one package of any kind of cookie dough (or have someone help you make a batch of cookie dough). Press the dough into a  round pizza pan and bake according to directions until cookie is done. Decorate the giant cookie like a gingerbread man's head with candy and colored frosting.